The person we know as Santa Claus in America and Britain orginated in Europe, where he is depicted differently in various countries, depending on their religious traditions.

In much of Europe, the kind man who distributes gifts during the Christmas season is known as Saint Nicholas. He was a bishop who lived in the fourth century at Myra, in what is now Turkey. According to legend, Nicholas was a wealthy man, known for his love of children and his acts of generosity to people less fortunate than himself.

His birthday, December 6, is celebrated in many European countries. On Saint Nicholas Day, children set out their shoes and he fills them with treats. In Belgium he rides a donkey, and the children leave hay and carrots by the fireplace. In the Netherlands he arrives by sea in a ship, and parades through town on a white horse. He often comes with a companion who carries the presents for well-behaved children, but he gives birch switches to children who have been naughty.

First published in the United States, Great Britain, Canada,
Australia, and New Zealand in 1995 by North-South Books,
an imprint of Nord-Süd Verlag AG, Gossau Zürich, Switzerland.

Copyright © 1994 by Nord-Süd Verlag AG, Gossau Zürich, Switzerland
First published in Switzerland under the title *Ein Geschenk vom Nikolaus*
English translation copyright © 1995 by North-South Books Inc.

Distributed in the United States by North-South Books Inc., New York.

Library of Congress Cataloging-in-Publication Data
Lachner, Dorothea.
[Geschenk vom Nikolaus. English]
The gift from Saint Nicholas / by Dorothea Lachner;
illustrated by Maja Dukíková; translated by J. Alison James.
Translation of: Ein Geschenk vom Nikolaus
Summary: When two children appeal to Saint Nicholas
to free their village from the heavy snow that is keeping
everyone inside, he sends instead a mysterious parcel.
[1. Saint Nicholas Day—Fiction.   2. Snow—Fiction]
I. Dusíková, Maja, ill.   II. Title
PZ7.L1353G1 1995
[E]—dc20 95-953

A CIP catalogue record for this book
is available from The British Library.

ISBN 1-55858-456-0 (trade binding)
1 3 5 7 9 TB 10 8 6 4 2
ISBN 1-55858-457-9 (library binding)
1 3 5 7 9 LB 10 8 6 4 2
Printed in Belgium

The Gift from Saint Nicholas

BY Dorothea Lachner

ILLUSTRATED BY Maja Dusíková

TRANSLATED BY J. ALISON JAMES

North-South Books

NEW YORK · LONDON

It had been snowing for over a week. Day after day, night after night. The wind had blown high snow mountains against the houses, and the village was white, and cold, and silent.

At first the villagers tried to keep the streets and paths cleared. But the snow kept falling, faster and faster, heavier and heavier. Finally everyone gave up. No one came to buy the shopkeeper's groceries or the baker's bread. The postman couldn't deliver any mail. Mrs. Kramer's back ached, but she couldn't get to the doctor. And Grandfather Gregor sat alone in his warm kitchen, wishing that his grandchildren could visit.

Since the villagers could do nothing, they just stayed in their houses and watched the snow pile higher and higher.

Anna and Misha watched too. They blew peepholes in the ice flowers on the window and stared out at the storm. It was Saint Nicholas Eve, and the children were worried.

"I'm tired of being trapped inside," said Misha. "Saint Nicholas Day won't be any fun if we can't get out to see Grandfather Gregor or any of our friends. If only Saint Nicholas would blow a path through the snow!"

"Then let's wish for it," said Anna. "On Saint Nicholas Eve, if you wish hard enough, whatever you wish for is supposed to come true." So they shut their eyes and sent their wish out through the peepholes in the ice.

The wish flew past barns and sheds, between the bare lilacs, out across the fields, and into the woods. It flew through spruce and cedar and pine and up a hill, where it landed on Saint Nicholas's beard. And from his beard to his ear it was just a short hop.

Saint Nicholas listened to the wish and nodded.

He went into his storeroom to choose the gifts for the villagers. "Apples, nuts, chocolate, and toys are not what the villagers need most this year," he mumbled to himself. "Gingerbread? No. Not even rocking horses or nutcrackers. This year is different. They need something special."

He searched and searched through the entire storeroom until he found it. It was an old thing, not much to look at. But it was exactly right.

In a flurry of rustling papers and crackling ribbons, he wrapped the shabby old thing. He packed it well.

Then Saint Nicholas pulled on his mittens, tied on his scarf, strapped on his skis, and set out.

Silently he sped down the hill, past pine and cedar and spruce, out across the field, between the bare lilacs, and into the sleeping village.

Anna and Misha heard a strange noise and woke up. Was there someone outside? They raced to the window.

"Look what Saint Nicholas brought!" whispered Anna.

In the middle of the village square stood a big, dark, mysterious sack.

Soon the people in the other houses also noticed the
mysterious sack.

"What could it be?"

"Who is it for?"

"Is it for me?"

Curious, they grabbed their shovels and began to dig paths through the snow. They shovelled snow for anyone who was too old or too weak. The children helped too. They all laughed and called to each other as they dug their way towards the sack in the middle of the square.

Shovelling made them warm. With rosy cheeks they stood around the sack and chattered excitedly.

"It could be a baby elephant!" said Misha.

"No, that's crazy!" said Anna

"It must be an oven," said the baker.

"Or a cask of raspberry juice," said the shopkeeper.

"Better that it be cough syrup," offered the doctor.

"A sack full of hay!" suggested Grandfather Gregor.

"Oh no, it is certainly a parcel," said the postman.

A child sighed. "I hope it's a doll—a huge doll that can dance and sing."

"Let's just open it and find out!" said Misha.

So they did.

Inside the sack was a huge package, gift-wrapped and tied with a bow. Under the paper there was a box. Inside the box was a slightly smaller package, also wrapped and tied with a bow. And inside that box another! The paper crackled; the ribbons waved; the boxes got smaller and smaller. The villagers laughed as they unwrapped each box. At last all there was left was a small, plain package.

"This present isn't big enough for us all to share," murmured the villagers, disappointed. "What a lot of work for nothing."

But they unwrapped it, with the children crouching and the adults peering curiously over their shoulders.

"A *teapot!*" they cried, astonished. "What good is a teapot?"

"A teapot is good for making tea," suggested Anna.

"Yes," agreed Grandfather Gregor. "We'll brew some tea. You may all come to my house. It's nice and warm in my kitchen."

The pot held enough tea for everyone. The baker sliced some fresh bread; the grocer laid out apples and tarts. Anna and Misha brought their old nutcracker and a basket of nuts. The doctor gave Mrs. Kramer some medicine that eased her aching back. The postman blew a peephole in the ice flowers on the window.

"We should send Saint Nicholas a thank-you letter," he said.

And Grandfather Gregor sat smiling, for now his warm kitchen was filled with people.

On their way home, Misha said to Anna: "You know, this turned out to be a wonderful Saint Nicholas Day after all!"

"Yes," said Anna. "And we *did* get our wish. Saint Nicholas may not have blown a path through the snow, but he did find a way to bring us all together!"